Captain Kindness

A pirate adventure of love,
compassion, family
...and vampires

Alex Mair

TSL Publications

First published in Great Britain in 2022
By TSL Publications, Rickmansworth

Copyright © 2022 Alex Mair

ISBN: 978-1-915660-15-2

The right of Alex Mair to be identified as the author of this work has been asserted by the author in accordance with the UK Copyright, Designs and Patents Act 1988.

All characters and events in this publication, other than those clearly in the public domain, are fictitious and any resemblance to actual persons, living or dead, is purely coincidental.

All rights reserved. No part of this publication may be reproduced, stored in a retrieval system or transmitted, in any form or by any means without the prior written permission of the publisher, nor be otherwise circulated in any form of binding or cover other than that in which it is published and without a similar condition being imposed on the subsequent buyer.

Cover courtesy of : Deveo Studio

For Gabriella,

without whom twice as much would've been written

in half the time.

Part One

One

Once upon a time, in a land far, far away, there was a happy town by the coast. It wasn't a dull country village surrounded by green and brown patchwork fields like the kind of place where children grow up all over England, this was a village where magic and the real world mixed together and nobody thought it was unusual. In the wild places beyond the town, you could find ogres and fairies and fire-breathing dragons. It was a dangerous world indeed, but in this town everyone was safe and happy. The happiest member of this village was Bella, the daughter of the lady who ran the local tavern, The Bell.

Bella was eleven and three quarters, and the most spirited girl in the entire town. Bella wouldn't go to bed on time, and snuck downstairs to steal chocolate from the cupboard in the middle of the night. Bella frequently thought she got away with it, but her parents always knew what she was up to. She could also be grumpy when she had chores to do around the house which she didn't want to do. But Bella had a different side to her. She could also be a headstrong and confident girl, who many times stood up to bullies in the playground, and who wasn't afraid to answer back to adults. This confidence made the other boys and girls want to trust her.

Her mother put this down to the fact that they lived without her father. Her mother always said the absence of her father meant that Bella had to grow up very quickly. Which is why she talked back to adults, who were frequently shocked that this little girl would give them lectures on how they should behave. She could stand her ground too. The other boys and girls loved it when she put the school terror, Raymond, in his place. Raymond's behaviour was frequently appalling, but Bella stood up to him.

Bella loved her mother. She grew to love her more and more

as she grew older. Bella saw how hard her mother worked to earn them a living and put a roof over their heads. Her mother worked long and hard at The Bell, serving ale to the sailors travelling with the British navy to the Caribbean. She served pies to the fishermen who worked at sea from dawn until dusk. For the rest of her life, the smell of freshly baked pies immediately took Bella back to The Bell which was always filled with the smell of her mother's pies, tarts, and flans.

It was a happy life in the town. There were no fields and meadows for the children to play in because the wilds beyond the town were filled with great beasts who would eat the children if they left after dusk. The favourite place for the children to play was on the cobbled streets, which criss-crossed the town from top to bottom. Bella's favourite time of day was twilight when the sun was setting but it was still light. Bella loved the glow of the street lamps in the twilight. She felt particularly proud of them because she had persuaded a town councillor to change the source of fuel from whale oil to vegetable, which was better for the environment and better for the ocean, which Bella loved.

Autumn turned into winter, and winter turned into spring. Fishermen continued to eat their pies and Bella's mother continued to serve ale in The Bell. The life of the town just went on; the women continued to gossip on market day and the old men played chess in the town square. The vicar continued to preach every Sunday morning. One day, the vicar wasn't watching where he placed his hand and fell out of the pulpit and onto the floor. The vicar landed on his bottom and fell backwards, so all the children caught a glimpse underneath the vicar's cassock. Bella, who was sitting at the back, caught a glimpse of the vicar's bright red underpants. Bella and all the other children laughed and laughed and laughed. The vicar blushed bright red like a rhubarb.

One day everything changed.

That was the day the pirates came.

The first sign was a cold wind coming in from the east. The

night-watchman was lazy, and frequently fell asleep on duty, despite it being his job to be on the lookout for danger all night.

The night-watchman suddenly felt very cold and wasn't sure why. 'Shouldn't be this cold in the middle of April,' he said to himself, wrapping his long coat closer to his chest, 'feels like December and where did that fog come from?'

At that moment he realised he was surrounded by a dense mist. The night-watchman realised it had descended on the town without warning. 'What in blue blazes is going on?' he said, scratching his bald head. He was afraid.

He poured more vegetable oil on the lamp, to get a better look over the harbour. As the light went up and he got a better view, he looked out and saw the vision of A GIGANTIC PIRATE SHIP!

Two

The great ship moved into the harbour. It was as wide as a football stadium and as tall as twelve double-decker busses stacked one on top of the other. The great ship towered over the village. The day after the invasion, the local newspaper published reports saying some villagers in the lower houses thought that the moon had disappeared, because the ugly black sails obscured and blacked out the moon. Other villagers reported a strange, cracking sound which was later discovered to be the hull of the ship breaking in low tide.

Bella woke up from her dream and went to the window. She saw the ugly black sails and the disgusting rotting wood that made up the body of the ship.

'Oh, my word!' she said. 'The old men of the sea weren't lying when they said how ugly the pirates were. That ship is revolting.' Bella was sure she saw a figure walking up and down the poop deck of the ship in a long dark coat and a wide hat. The captain? she wondered to herself.

'Bella!' screeched her mother. 'It's not safe here. You must get below ground NOW!'

Bella knew instantly what she meant. There was a trapdoor in the kitchen behind the bar of The Bell which led to the cellar. The cellar was used to keep the barrels loaded with rum for the sailors of the British Navy. Bella knew it well because sometimes she and the other boys and girls from school used to play there during half-term, when the adults were not around. Or at least when they thought the adults were not around, sometimes she would hear the sound of her mother shouting at a drunken sailor. They would realise there were grownups around and run away.

On one occasion, Bella was playing with Raymond in the cellar. Raymond, who had recently been given a poor end of term report, felt the need to take it out on somebody else and decided to lock Bella in the dark cellar all by herself. Raymond told Bella that he was just going to get something-or-other and would be right back. Bella stayed there for what seemed like ages, before her mother finally rescued her. 'Bella, what on earth have you been doing down there?' she asked. Mum was shocked at the sight of a tear-stained Bella hugging herself for comfort. Bella explained that this was Raymond's idea of a 'joke', and her mother then went over to Raymond's house and gave Raymond and his parents the biggest ticking-off Bella had ever seen.

The pirates were close by now. With her mother's help, Bella made her way downstairs from her bedroom to the cellar. She could've sworn she heard explosions which she took to be cannon-fire and the sound of men at arms running in the direction of the harbour. Bella was scared.

Oh, I don't care what you do, just don't hurt my mum Bella thought to herself as she lowered herself down into the cellar.

Bella was confused when her mother paused at the top of the stairs.

'Mum, come down! It's dangerous!' shouted Bella.

'I'm not coming with you,' said her mother.

Bella felt suddenly very frightened; 'but what will you do? Those nasty pirates...'

'I can take care of myself Bella, you just stay down here in the cellar and don't move, are you listening?'

'Yes Mum,' said Bella. With that her mother said she was a good girl and closed the cellar door.

Bella had never quite trusted people after the wretched Raymond locked her in the cellar all alone in the dark. Mum said it was because Raymond had been locked in a cellar all alone by his father. Feeling humiliated, Raymond decided to take it out on somebody else. Bella felt concerned, but strangely confident in her mother. My mummy is a tough woman, Bella thought to herself. She loved her mother, who had brought her up all on her own after her father was no longer around. If there is anyone in the world who can see off those pirates it would be

her mother, Bella thought to herself.
There was a moment's silence, which to Bella felt like forever.
Then the doors of The Bell swung open, and Bella heard the first footsteps of the Pirates on the hard, wooden floor of the tavern. She thought to herself; they're here.

Three

The Pirate Captain strode into the bar of The Bell. Mum stood behind the bar, with her hands pressed on the counter, as if to say, you don't scare me Pirate Captain. It would've taken a very clever pirate to see through her; underneath Mum was terrified that the Pirates would find her little girl below stairs, but she would stand firm. She wouldn't show fear. She wouldn't give the Pirate Captain the pleasure of that.

Slowly, the Pirate Captain took a small, immaculate gold device from the inside pocket of his handsome red overcoat. He wore a large black hat and posh leather boots. Mum instantly recognized it as some kind of pocket watch. It had a remarkably detailed surface and must have cost a fortune to make. The Pirate Captain took the pocket watch and examined the position of the spidery hands.

'Good evening, my good woman,' said the Pirate Captain. The Pirate Captain always spoke to women and girls like this, to give the impression that he was relaxed around women, which really, he wasn't.

'It's fifteen minutes before closing time and my men are thirsty,' he said. He gestured to the other members of the crew behind him; 'Six ales and some shepherd's pie please.'

'You'll get nothing but a door in your face and a cold walk back to ship, Captain. I don't let pirates into my Inn. Let alone Pirates who scare the living daylights out of my village. Now clear off!'

Bella suddenly felt a feeling well up inside her. It was pride, listening to her mother telling the Pirate Captain to clear off with courage and confidence. The Pirate Captain suddenly looked very sad; 'But my dear lady, don't you know who I am?'

Mum looked puzzled. 'No...should I?'

'I am Captain Greed, the most feared and deadly Pirate on the high seas,' he said, beaming a massive grin.

'Oh, right,' said Mum, very unimpressed. 'Well, Mr Pirate Greed, the-most-feared-and-deadly-Pirate-on-the-high-seas, perhaps you can tell me why you are here and what you want.'

'Oh, it's very simple really,' he said. 'I just want the contents of your till and the deeds to your Inn. Hand them over.'

'And what if I refuse?' asked Mum.

'Then we'll arrest you and put you in the Brigg. Then... err...we'll take your Inn anyway.'

Bella gasped. For god's sake just do as he says, she thought. Bella was so nervous she began shuffling on the spot. Taking a step backwards, she accidentally knocked over an empty bucket. The noise of the bucket falling was loud enough to be heard upstairs

'What was that noise?' demanded the Pirate Captain.

'Oh, nothing,' said Mum' 'Err...listen, before I hand over my only home to you Captain Greed, answer me this question: What's so special about The Bell? Why do you want it?'

'Oh, nothing,' he said. 'My crew are just thirsty. I don't need your home and business, but since we're here, I might as well take it anyway.'

'Well then you are a greedy and cruel man, Captain,' said Mum. 'You can't have it. So there.'

'LOCK HER UP!' roared Captain Greed. Two men emerged from behind Greed. Together they clasped Mum in chains. Bella felt a rising sense of anger and injustice: 'How DARE they do that!' she thought to herself silently.

'Captain Greed, before you throw me onto your ship, answer me this...Why are you taking my tavern if you don't need it? This is the only home I have. Surely you can take pity on a good, decent, hard-working mother and her daughter?' said Mum. Bella felt a tear develop in her eye.

The Pirate Captain laughed so hard his hat nearly fell off; 'My good woman, it's really simple actually. I absolutely love gold. I love everything about it. I love the smell of it. I love the texture of it. I love its colour. The only thing I truly love in the whole wide world is gold, gold, gold. I love gold so much I became a landlord. I already own eleven properties on the Spanish Main and am a millionaire. I've made myself a fortune. Everyone can become a millionaire, as long as they are hard-working and apply themselves. It's easy, you see. I don't care if you lose your home. Perhaps if you spent less time eating pies with the old men of the sea and more time saving your money, you would be rich too.'

As she was being led out of the tavern and into the night air where fate waited her on the Pirate ship, Mum thought Captain Greed was very silly as well as selfish. 'Then you are most unkind Captain Greed and you deserve everything you get,' she said.

'Come on boys,' said Captain Greed. 'Let's help ourselves to as much ale as we can drink and as much rich food as we can eat before we set sail,' and a great shout went up from the crew as the pirates roared for rum. At that point, Bella decided she'd had enough.

Four

'NO!' cried Bella as she threw open the door to the cellar and burst into the room. The pirates turned to look in amazement.

'Who on earth are you little girl?' asked Captain Greed.

'My name is Bella and this is my mother. I'm telling you to stop being mean to her, turn around and go away!'

Captain Greed looked stunned in amazement. 'Well, I have never been spoken to like that before...' he said.

'...explains a lot,' said Bella.

'MEN!' cried Captain Greed, 'put her in arms!'

Two men emerged from behind Captain Greed's long dark coat. With their strong arms they took Bella's hands and placed them in chains.

'Right, just for that remark, little girl, I'm going to give you a choice. Either your mother can surrender your home...'

'And what exactly will you do with our home? Yes, our home?' said Bella

'What will I do with it?' said the Pirate Captain, suddenly looking like the thought had only just come to him there and then. 'I'll sell it and become even richer than I am now!'

'And what exactly will become of me, my mother and our dog?'

'Oh, I don't care, go out on the road or something, or... wait!?!...did you say you have a dog?'

'Yes, we have a dog. Her name is Coco,' said Bella.

'You didn't tell me you have a dog,' said the Pirate Captain, suddenly looking very frightened. 'Dogs are unhygienic, smelly and noisy.'

'A bit like your pirate ship then?' said Bella interrupting the Pirate Captain in mid-sentence.

'Shut up little girl!' snapped the Pirate Captain.

'Dogs chew everything in sight, wee everywhere and stink to high heaven. I don't want them anywhere near a property of mine,' said the Pirate Captain.

Bella rolled her eyes. 'What kind of pets do landlords like you expect us to own in a small flat above a pub...a dragon!?!' said Bella. Now she was cross with being told what to do by a rich pirate who thought it somehow his right to charge into their home whenever he wants. She thought to herself, what gives him the right to have it all his own way?'

'What's wrong with dogs anyway?' asked Bella.

'I loathe dogs. I hate them. I've had them on my crew before now and it was a disaster, also I'm allergic to them. If I go anywhere near a dog I start to cough, sneeze and I get the most terrible headaches.'

'Well, Captain, I have some bad news for you because this dog gets everywhere. There are hairs on every chair, on every stool, on every piece of furniture in this tavern. I'm sorry, you'll have to turn around and go home. We'll also take back our home thank you very much.'

'As I was saying girl,' shouted the Pirate Captain. 'I was going to offer you a choice. Either a) you and your mother give your tavern to me, and I'll let the pair of you go or b) I kidnap you and your mother, then I will sell your tavern anyway. That's only after my crew and I help ourselves to as much rum as we can fit on the ship without drowning in the harbour.'

Bella thought the Pirate Captain was the cruellest, meanest person she had ever, ever met. How dare this pirate think their home as his property just because he's rich.

'THAT'S NOT A CHOICE!' shouted Bella. 'I'm sorry Captain, but I'm not going with you. We are staying right here. We're not going anywhere.'

'Well, we'll see about that. Mr Higgins if you please...!' shouted the Captain.

A tall man with a very long face emerged. He was wearing a blue jacket and had a small pair of round spectacles balancing on his nose. 'This is Mr Higgins,' said Captain Greed. 'He's in charge of the accounts section of the ship.'

'Mr Higgins, please read the prisoners their rights according to the Pirate code.'

Mr Higgins pulled out a paper scroll, turned to Bella, adjusted his round spectacles so they sat comfortably on the bridge of his nose, coughed twice and read from the top: 'In accordance with article one, clause four, sub-section thirty-six of the founding document of the Pirate Charter, I hereby apprehend your dwelling and all its belongings and consign Bella and her mother, to a life of servitude on the ship. Your mother will be put in irons and put in the brig. You, Bella, will be put to work, mopping the deck and serving the crew their grog. Your night duties will include sitting in the crow's nest all night, on the lookout for enemy ships. For these tasks, you will be paid a little bit of money but not much. Only on making the princely sum of one thousand doubloons, may you and your mother be released from captivity.'

Bella gulped.

'Take them to the brig, Mr Higgins!' bellowed Captain Greed. 'Men! The bar is open! Help yourself to whatever you want!'

Bella and her mother were officially prisoners of Captain Greed and his crew. As they were being led out of The Bell and towards the harbour, Bella could hear villagers crying. The church bells were ringing to indicate alarm. Irons were placed on her mother's wrists and Mr Higgins, accompanied by the crew, led the pair out of the tavern and down towards the sea in the direction of the great ship.

As they were being led down the cobbled streets under the moonlight. Bella recognised the smell of sea salt in the air, and out of the corner of her eye, glimpsed pirates stealing chests of gold onto the belly of the vast ship. Bella saw that her mum had tears in her eyes.

'I'm sorry, Bella,' said Mum.

'It's alright,' Bella said. 'We're going to be ok.' Bella looked at her mother and felt filled with love that she had been given such a clear, direct show of love that many other boys and girls in the village had probably never experienced.

Five

It was night. The great ship didn't stop. Behind the ship's wheel, Captain Greed stared at the horizon. He lit a candle for more light. He opened the pocket of his long coat and took out a beautiful gold compass. Its hands told him they were heading west.

'Starboard-ho!' cried Captain Greed. The crew of the ship pulled at the ropes hanging from the top of the great, black rotting sails. The ship took a sharp turn to the right, and the ship continued through the giant waves.

Bella spent most of her time at night in the crow's nest. Coco the dog couldn't come on the pirate ship, so one of the old men of the sea who was a regular at The Bell, and who Mum trusted completely, offered to look after her until Bella and her mother returned. If they returned.

When Bella and her mum were brought in irons on-board the ship, the Captain said, 'You girls are going to be held in the brig, that's the ship's prison. The brig is only for the worst, most treacherous criminals on board; mutineers, spies and thieves. This will be your home now, so get used to it.' Bella and Mum were led down into the belly of the great ship to see the brig, and when they saw it they were appalled. In front of them was a row of cells with iron bars and a large iron lock on the front. In the cells were nothing except a bed of straw, a slop bucket and a small window to the outside world. Mum wanted to cry but Bella knew she had to be strong.

As they were being given a brief tour of the ship on their way to the brig, Bella was amazed at what she saw. Each new room had new treasures. Bella couldn't believe her eyes.

On the deck, waiting to go down, Bella was stunned to see a parade of Oompa-Loompas scrubbing the deck. Bella gazed upwards at the crow's nest and saw through the criss-crossing ropes and pulleys, a team of munchkins working the rigging. In Captain Greed's quarters there was a large and splendid table, with wonderful gold armchairs, velvet curtains and a grand mahogany table. In the middle, a diamond candelabra with a diamond encrusted skull was sitting above the mantelpiece. Bella stood open-mouthed at the sight of the sparrow from The Happy Prince, sitting in a cage looking lonely. The Cheshire Cat warmed himself in front of the fireplace, and if it was feeling sociable, would rub noses with Toto, Dorothy's pet dog from Kansas, who was enjoying a big stretch on the carpet.

Descending into the belly of the ship, she noticed that decorating the walls of the ship were memorabilia the Captain had collected, each kept behind clear glass boxes of the kind that Bella had seen before, in museums her mother had taken her to in the village. Bella was stunned that one Pirate ship would have collected this much loot.

'Here you are,' said the guard, outside the brig. He pointed towards one cell. 'In you go,' said the disgusting pirate. Bella felt his horrible breath as he spoke. With that, Bella and Mum were thrown into the cell.

The first thing to do was to decide which one of them would get the bed. Because Bella was a kind girl, she offered the bed to her mother so she could rest her back. Mum protested that Bella needed the bed more, but Bella insisted her mother have the bed. When Greed found out about this arrangement, he couldn't understand it.

Their days were spent with the Oompa-Loompas and the munchkins toiling on the ship. Her mother spent her days sewing bedsheets for the crew and darning socks, while Bella worked the rigging, scrubbed the poop deck and re-painted the ship. The days were long and boring. Bella started to wonder if she and her mother would ever make it back home. She thought of the village and the old men of the sea and the smell of her mum's homemade shepherd's pie filling The Bell on a cold evening. I'm missing all that, she said to herself.

One evening Bella and Mum were tucking into their evening

meal of bread and cheese when her mum said; 'Bella, did Captain Greed give any indication of where we are going?'

'No,' said Bella.

'Maybe we should try and find out...' suggested Mum.

Suddenly there was a noise from the next cell. Bang...bang...bang...

'What was that?' said Bella.

'It sounded like it came from next door,' Mum replied.

Bella and her mum sat in silence and waited. BANG...BANG...BANG...

Bella put her ear to the wall and listened. 'It's coming through the walls!' she cried.

Bella sat and cuddled her mother. 'Mum, this thing coming through the wall is going to kill and eat us,' she said. They were both petrified. 'Goodbye, Bella. I love you!' said Mum.

Suddenly the horrible thing next door finally broke through the wall. There was a great explosion of dust and the stones holding together the wall collapsed, and suddenly - A GIANT DOG poked its head through the hole in the wall and said, 'Hello.'

'Hello?' said Bella.

'What's your name?' asked the dog.

'Bella, and this is my mother,' said Bella. 'Are you going to eat us?'

'No, I'm not going to eat you,' the dog replied. 'I don't eat fellow prisoners of Captain Greed.'

'Oh right. Nice to meet you. How do you do?' said Bella.

The dog was a bit puzzled. 'You are strangely dressed for pirates?' he said, looking at the blue jeans and trainers that Bella was wearing and her mother, dressed in a stripy top, emerald green cardigan and blue jeans.

'Excuse me?' said Bella.

'Pardon me?' replied the dog.

'Just who do you think you are?' replied Bella.

'Have I done something wrong?' asked the dog, suddenly looking very frightened.

'Oh,' said Bella. 'You mean apart from ruining our cell and scaring me and my mum half to death?'

'Oh,' said the dog. 'Sorry about that...'

'Perhaps some answers maybe in order,' said Bella.

'Very well. My name is D.O.G.G.I.E. Pronounced D-O-G-G-I-E. But you can call me Doggie.'

Bella looked and saw that Doggie was wearing a dog collar and attached to it was a long metal chain snaking back into his cell. The chain was attached to a pole coming out of the floor. Bella glimpsed over the pile of rubble that used to be the wall separating Doggie's cell from hers.

'Are you the ship's pet?' asked Bella.

'I wish,' said Doggie.

'What are you in for?' asked Bella. 'Did you bite the Captain's hand?'

'I wish I had done that too,' said Doggie. 'No, I'm in here for good old-fashioned mutiny I'm afraid.'

'What are you doing on the pirate ship?' asked Mum. 'I thought Captain Greed is allergic to dogs.'

'Oh, he is,' said Doggie, 'which is why I was hired as the navigator. We met each other very few times, I spent most of my time in the crow's nest looking through a telescope.'

'A bit like me...' said Bella.

'That's a nice way of looking at it,' said Doggie.

'What's all this about a mutiny?' said Bella.

'Well, you see, it's very arrogant of Captain Greed to assume that absolutely everybody shares his love of money. The Captain thinks that absolutely everyone can get rich if they just put their minds to it, but some of us on the crew know that's not true. The Captain can get rich from being a landlord and hoarding his gold out of sight. So some of us got together and decided we'd do away with Greed and run the ships ourselves.'

Bella, Doggie and Mum talked long into the night. They were lucky because the guard drank lots of rum, so he fell asleep quickly after lights out and didn't wake up again until dawn.

Doggie told them everything. Doggie had been employed as the ship's navigator, being a seven-foot-tall dog, his powerful nose was particularly useful for sniffing out enemy ships. He was also very good with maps and compasses, but it's not uncommon for dogs from his island to be seven-foot tall and good with maps and compasses.

Doggie and the other members of the crew had wanted the gold stolen by Greed to be given back to towns and villages on the coast. The Captain didn't like this idea. Together with the crew, Doggie decided to kidnap the Captain, take control of the ship, and redistribute the gold amongst the poor. They also planned to include the gold he had made from his houses. Not to mention the millions in gold he was hiding in Panama.

'But the plan didn't go too well,' said Doggie. 'The Captain escaped, retook his gold and we were all thrown in the brig.'

'What happened to them?' said Bella.

'They've all been made to walk the plank,' said Doggie. 'Today I'm the last of the mutineers left alive.'

'Oh, I'm sorry to hear that,' said Bella, feeling an overwhelming sadness. She knew that not every pirate was greedy.

'Oi! What's going on here!' enquired a voice in the darkness.

Disaster! thought Bella. The guard had been roused from his sleep. Bella heard the sound of leather boots on the floor. Sitting petrified, the three listened to the sound of the guard running in their direction.

'Hello,' said the guard raising his lamp to get a better look. 'What have we here? Three prisoners sharing the same cell...? Have you been trying to escape again, Doggie?'

Doggie said nothing, and just looked down at his paws in embarrassment.

'I thought so,' said the guard. 'Well, obviously, I'll have to report this to the Captain. You know what happened to the last prisoners who were disobedient.'

'No, we don't,' said Bella.

'They walked the plank. A toothsome snack for the sharks who swim in these oceans.'

Bella gulped hard. Oh dear, she thought.

The sun was rising over the ship. The maroon sky looked beautiful over the wine-dark sea. 'Yes', said the guard in a very self-satisfied voice. 'I see it's going to be a very beautiful day.'

Six

In the morning Bella, Mum and Doggie were due to walk the plank. One of Captain Greed's favourite things to do was to host a competition on the ship to see who amongst the crew could be the meanest, greediest, most unkind pirate and Captain Greed would award them the prize.

Every time a competition was announced, each member of the crew dutifully lined up to prove the depths of their selfishness and greed. But this competition was a fraud. In fact, Captain Greed had rigged the competition by speaking to the judges and promising to take away their grog if they voted 'the wrong way.'

Fifty times Greed had held the competition, and fifty times he won. It was the solemn responsibility for the crew to line up and congratulate the Captain on how brilliant he was. The following year, the fifty-first year in the award's history, the Captain decided that in celebration of how magnificent he was at his job, a special award would be founded, for modesty. After consulting with the crew, Greed decided that the inaugural Captain Greed Award for Modesty would be awarded to himself, because since Greed was obviously the most modest, the kindest and the most caring pirate on the Spanish main, it would be pointless to hold the competition, as Greed would win it anyway. Greed's final action in the story of the modesty award was to order the crew to work extra hours so the ship would be nice and clean for the award ceremony.

One of the crew's favourite topics of conversation was discussing what exactly the Captain did with all the treasure they had ransacked from villages, towns, the Royal Navy and other pirate ships. In the evening the crew and the Captain were having dinner. The crew was passing around the rum for the crew, and wine for the captain. 'Err...Captain,' started one of the younger members of the crew, 'what exactly do you do with all the treasure we've plundered?'

The Captain roared with laughter. Looking back on it, the younger member of the crew remembered feeling puzzled when the Captain laughed and laughed, but the other members of the crew looked petrified, and sat in stony silence.

'Oh, my dear fellow,' said the Captain, wiping dribbles of soup and wine out of his long, unkempt beard, 'what I do with the treasure, is exactly what you would expect a kind, caring and responsible Captain to do. I use it to make you richer.'

'You make us richer? The crew, you mean?' The young boy thought the Captain had gone quite mad. Was the Captain really suggesting that the point of all these daring raids was so the Captain could make them richer? 'But Captain, how do you do it?'

The Captain looked at the boy like he was a fool. 'It's simple really. I let a good friend of mine look after it.'

'You let a good friend look after it?'

'Yes, a good friend of mine called Gustav, a fellow Pirate on a different ship who advises Pirates, such as myself, on what to do with all the treasure we plunder.'

'I see,' said the young boy. 'May I ask Captain, since you are so clever and so very, very kind to be putting all this money away for us, how does it work? How do we get richer, I mean?'

'Oh, well, I stick all the treasure in a magic cave with a spell cast on it by the Wizard of Saint Esmeralda Island, which makes the pot of treasure grow bigger and bigger every year. Great, isn't it? When we've finished plundering every island in the Caribbean, we'll take out our treasure and will all be so rich we'll never have to set sail again. Brilliant.'

'A Wizard? A magic spell? Captain, have you been dabbling in the dark arts.'

'Don't worry my boy, my bank manager Gustav and his company - Gustav and Bones: commercial law, financial advice but definitely not tax evasion PLC - has nothing to hide. Gustav has written to me to assure me that the cave and the witch-doctor and the magic spell are all above board, and I have done nothing that would get us in trouble with the Royal Navy and their tax collectors.

'Oh...' said the young boy. 'Oh, I see.'

The sun was high over the masthead, meaning it was now noon - and that could only mean one thing; it was time for the condemned prisoners in the brig to walk the plank.

'Permission to bring out the prisoners, sir!' asked the guard who had been keeping watch over Brig.

'Permission granted!' cried the Captain.

And with that, Bella, Mum and Doggie were brought out. One by one, they stepped out from the belly of the lower decks and into the sunlight. Bella's eyes hurt in the sunlight and were blinded for a few moments, when her eyes calmed down, she couldn't believe what she saw; the entire crew had turned out; The Captain stood above everyone else just next to the wheel of the ship where his first mate was standing completely still. The great ship was at a standstill. There was no wind in the air, so all the sails of the ship were rolled up and the sun in the sky was violently hot.

'Stand over there,' pointed the guard.

Bella, her mother and Doggie moved over to the side of the ship. If Bella leaned back, she thought she would tip over into the sea.

'Do the prisoners have any last requests?' bellowed the Captain.

'Please Captain, I have one last request,' said Bella.

'Yes, what is it?'

'Can you undo these chains and let us go? That would be so very kind of you, thanks,' said Bella.

The Captain shook his head. 'Poor silly young woman, still arguing back to adults even now. Will you ever learn? Just for that outburst young lady, your mother can watch you walk the plank first.'

Bella looked at her mother. Her mother was fighting back the tears. Bella thought back to that evening when they were kidnapped from the tavern, and how she had told her mother it was going to be ok, and her tears had been a clear, direct show of love that the other children of the village had probably never seen. She wanted to say; 'I'm sorry Mum...' when suddenly Doggie burst forward and said, 'Captain...?'

'Yes, what do you have to say for yourself you treacherous mutt?'

'I feel that I should walk the plank first. Unlike this poor girl and her mother, I am the real villain here. The brig is harder for them than it is for me, because I'm used to the pirate life. On the other hand, I was given every luxury that comes with being a member of this crew. I was trusted by my fellow members of the crew and given responsibility, gold and three-square meals a day. And I betrayed that trust by starting a mutiny. So, in many ways, I should walk the plank first because I deserve it more.'

The crew looked a bit puzzled and glanced at one another as if to say, what on earth is this seven-foot dog up to?

'Doggie,' said Bella, 'have you gone stark raving mad?'

'First rule of friendship Bella,' said Doggie, 'when you are in a tight spot, always put the people you love before yourself. Love them.'

'Well, what about it Captain?' said Doggie.

The Captain remained silent for a few moments and said, 'Alright then. Off you go.'

Gingerly, Doggie out on foot on the plank. The entire crew stood open-mouthed in silence. Bella saw a parrot's eyes pop out of its head in astonishment.

Doggie walked slowly towards the plank. Stood, feet together, towards the end of the plank. Bent down, and in one motion, jumped high into the air and dived like a swan into the sea. Splash! Bella peered over the side of the ship to glance at Doggie's dive. There was a white foam where Doggie's huge body had disturbed the surface of water, and he sank beneath the waves.

'Right. Excellent. Good,' said the Captain, feeling very smug. 'Now for the rest of those treacherous dogs!'

Bella hugged her mother tight.

'Goodbye Mum,' said Bella.

'Captain,' said Bella's mother, 'if my beloved daughter and I are going to walk the plank, let us do it together. Please, it's a mother's request.'

The Captain thought for a moment, 'Alright, go on then.'

With that, Bella and her mother put one foot on the plank. Mum was nearly halfway up the plank when she suddenly noticed that Bella was reluctant. 'Mum...I don't want to go.'

Bella's mother tried to hold her crying daughter.

On board the ship, one particularly impatient pirate grew bored. 'This is sooooo boring,' he said. And with one swift motion of his foot, kicked the plank away.

Bella and Mum went flying down into the sea. They crashed through the waves and a great cheer went up from the crew on board. Captain Greed immediately gave the instructions to turn the ship around and set sail in the opposite direction, where they were going to raid a governor's house in Jamaica.

Bella and her mother clung to each other as the waves crashed around them. Bella thought this was the end and tried to say goodbye Mum but suddenly...

Bella became aware of something coming up from the deep. There was a great commotion from below and Bella became aware of something hard and wet underneath her feet...

DOGGIE!

'Bella! Mum! Quick, hold on to my ears!'

Bella and her mother gripped tightly onto the animal's ears. Because Doggie was so huge, and his ears were so big, it meant that Bella and her mother could hold on and each ear would act like a lido. 'Doggie, you're the greatest, how did you do it?' asked Bella.

'It's simple really, I used my enormous lungs to hold my breath underneath the water for long enough until the ship had moved on. Then I rose to the surface to save you.'

'Doggie, I think you are the greatest friend ever,' said Bella.

The two women held tightly onto Doggie's ears and the creature used his enormous muscles to swim hard through the seas. 'First rule of piracy Bella - when you are in a tight spot, trick 'em.'

Part Two

Seven

On they went, swimming on and on through the waters. Bella was exhausted but very happy. Doggie had outwitted Captain Greed and his crew. They were on their way to safety. When asked where they were going, Doggie informed them that he knew of an island near to where they had all been made to walk the plank. Doggie had criss-crossed these waters many times. Many times, he saw Captain Greed gazing at the island with a sad expression on his face, but he didn't know why.

The island was certainly a lonely place. Shrouded by a thick dense fog, a giant mountain rose out of the middle and near the beach, was a thick jungle forest. As the party swam closer towards the beach, and the island came closer and closer, Bella started to wonder where she was. The jungle beyond the white sandy beach looked like the kind she had imagined the rain forest to be; bustling with creepy crawlies, snakes, pythons and maybe a tiger or two. But the fog was not at all tropical. It was a thick fog, like the kind that falls on the English countryside in winter. The fog made her think of England at the time of the Doomsday Book, which she had been learning about in school. What on earth has Doggie got us into? she thought to herself.

The party landed on the beach. Mum and Bella let go of Doggie and stepped off his shoulders and onto the beach. Doggie immediately did that thing dogs always do when they have been for a dip in the sea, which is to have a full body shake. Bella and her mother were both covered in seawater.

'Silly dog,' said Mum.

It was late afternoon. The sun was still hot although it was lower in the sky now. Captain Greed's ship was now nothing more than a distant memory. 'It will be dark soon, we'll have to start a fire,' said Mum.

'I'll gather the rocks and arrange them in a circle,' said Bella, 'but first...'

And with that, Bella and her mother broke out in laughter and began singing and dancing with great joy. They had escaped Captain Greed. Bella, Mum and Doggie all ran up and down the length of the beach, kicking sand in the air and saying how happy they were. They continued to play and be happy and danced and danced and danced and danced.

Their laughter and cries of joy must have been very loud indeed because suddenly they heard a deep booming voice coming from the jungle's edge; 'What are you doing here?' said the voice.

The party spun round.

'Who dares to enter this Island?' demanded the voice.

'Who is that?' said Mum.

'I really don't know,' said Doggie.

'Whoever he is he looks quite scary,' added Bella.

A man stood on the head of the beach, just at the jungle's edge. Bella struggled for a moment to see, as the man was carrying a huge sword, which reflected the sunlight, blinding Bella for a few moments. Bella saw two eyes staring out at her from underneath a black hood. The man was clothed but Bella couldn't see exactly what he was wearing because wrapped around him was a large robe. Bella could see he had lots of bracelets on. He had a nice beard. Not the foul-smelling, unkempt beard, like the kind Captain Greed wore. His beard was tidy, well-managed.

'What are you doing here?' asked the stranger.

'We have escaped from Captain Greed,' said Doggie. 'We have come to seek refuge on this island.'

'Have you indeed?' said the stranger.

'Yes,' said Bella. 'We need your help to get us home. We need directions on how to return home.'

'You three are just lucky I don't kill you right here and now,' said the man.

The trio looked shocked. They weren't expecting this kind of person.

'Just who are you?' asked Bella.

'My name is Luigi,' said the man, 'and I guard this island.'

'Just what are you doing here?' said Bella.

'I make sure this island remains undisturbed by pirates, smugglers and spies,' said Luigi.

'Ah, I see,' said Bella, 'so there is obviously something on this island worth protecting. Something hidden? Something valuable?' Bella looked into Luigi's sad eyes which peered at her from underneath his dark hood. Suddenly she had a thought: 'I know, something secret.'

'You are very clever girl,' said Luigi.

'That's my daughter,' said Mum. 'She is clever, kind to animals, she loves science and is doing very well in school. She loves her mother and is not afraid to speak her mind. Watch out though, this little one has a sharp tongue.'

'There is something secret hidden on this island, isn't there?' said Bella, suddenly realizing that she was excited.

'I can see that you are an unusually perceptive little girl,' said Luigi, 'Pleased to meet you.'

Bella put one hand out to shake Luigi's hand. Luigi stood still like a statue. 'Aren't you going to shake my hand?' said Bella.

'I'm afraid I can't do that,' said Luigi.

'Why not?' said Bella.

'I'm sensitive to sunlight,' said Luigi.

'I'm sensitive to sunlight too,' said Bella.

'Not like me,' said Luigi. Bella looked confused. What on earth could he mean? she wondered.

'I'll show you. I can't take my hood off but if you come and have a look at the side of my neck, you'll be able to see it.' So Bella moved in for a closer look. There on the side of his neck was the thing that Luigi was trying to hide, two red puncture marks on the side of his neck.

'You're a vampire!?!' said Bella. 'But what are you doing here, on this island? In the middle of the day?'

'This island has been my home for centuries since I moved here hundreds of years ago,' said Luigi. 'I am part of an ancient vampire class. Over centuries we've been hunted down by pirates. Now, I am the last of my kind.'

'So, you're really old?' said Bella.

'Yes, I'm 395 years old,' said Luigi.

'And you live here all alone,' said Bella.

'Well not quite alone...' said Luigi, looking into the distance. 'But this island is a good place to avoid unwanted attention, if you know what I mean. Look the sun is going down.'

The four gazed at the horizon. The sun was going down and the sky had turned red. Soon the sun would go down and Bella knew they were in trouble. They were stuck on a deserted island, with a vampire, and no chance of help. She faced a choice, to trust Luigi or not.

'Luigi, we need your help. We're all alone and we need shelter for the night and safe passage off the island. Can you help us?' said Bella.

'I can give you shelter for the night,' said Luigi, 'but I can't get you off the island. Only she has the power.'

'And who is she?' enquired Bella.

'Oh don't worry about that for now, you'll find out soon enough. Come with me.'

'So, what?' said Mum, 'we are just supposed to trust you? We know nothing about you.'

'Come with me, and I will tell my tale.'

Eight

They went up from the beach and into the jungle. The four marched single file through the thick, dense forest. Luigi led the party from the front, hacking through thick undergrowth with his enormous blade. Bella and Mum were amazed at the strength of this 395-year-old vampire; he just kicked logs aside like they were twigs. He was careful though never to let the sunlight catch his bare skin in case it burnt him to a crisp. Bella noticed they were walking uphill.

'Where are we going?' asked Bella.

'To visit her,' said Luigi.

'Her?' queried Mum,

'She who is queen of this island, the most important person on it by far, the oldest and wisest person on this island, the witch-doctor.'

'A witch-doctor?' said Mum.

'Yes, the witch-doctor. She will give us food and shelter for the night and tomorrow we will work out our next move against Captain Greed,' said Luigi, thrusting his blade down towards a thick branch and cutting it in half.

'Do you hear that, Bella? We are going to see the witch-doctor?' said Mum.

'I'm not sure how I feel about this,' said Bella.

'Well do you have a better idea? Should we just wait on the beach for the rest of time? Maybe you would prefer swimming out to Captain Greed's ship and having a better time there,' said Mum.

Bella wondered if this Luigi vampire was completely trustworthy. Perhaps he had a hidden agenda. Maybe he would take them up to the top of the island and kill them. Maybe he would cut them up and feed them to the fish that swim in the waters around the island.

'We're almost there,' said Luigi.

'Look, there. That's where she lives,' said Luigi pointing his cutlass forward.

'I can't see,' said Bella pushing past Doggie, who was beginning to smell because his fur was covered in seawater. He needed a good bath.

'Here let me show you,' said Luigi. 'Come closer.' He motioned her towards him, and with one swift movement of his blade lifted a curtain of low hanging vines.

The sun burst through blinding Bella for a few seconds, but she looked down and finally, she saw there was a spot of low land, away from the jungle's edge. A low-lying meadow which was protected from the wind and the rain. In the middle of the meadow was a ramshackle old dwelling which resembled little more than a woodman's cottage which had fallen into disrepair. In the front garden of the cottage there was a bench outside with a figure in black sitting on it. Bella saw the figure, which she knew instantly to be the witch-doctor, clutching a walking stick with her wrinkled hands.

'There she is. She's been expecting us,' said Luigi.

'How does she know we're coming?' said Bella.

'She specialises in the unexpected,' said Luigi. 'Come along, not far now. Hold hands, it's very steep on the way down.'

Nine

The party walked single file down towards the meadow, holding hands as they went. Bella held her mother's hand tightly; she could tell that she was both excited and a bit nervous. Eventually, the four - Bella, Mum, Doggie and Luigi - made their way down to the cottage where the witch-doctor was waiting for them.

The final challenge before meeting the witch-doctor was the bogs. 'Be careful everyone,' said Luigi, 'don't fall into the bogs.'

Bella looked up at the sky. Suddenly she felt very scared. In the time it had taken them to walk from the jungle's edge towards the lowlands, the sky had transformed from a bright blue into a swirl of grey and black clouds.

Luigi approached the elderly lady sitting on the bench, clutching her walking stick in her hands.

'Good afternoon, old lady,' said Luigi.

'Good afternoon? It is almost evening my child,' said the witch-doctor. Doggie and Bella were hiding behind Mum. Bella peeked around Mum's legs. The witch-doctor wore a black cowl, like a monk. Bella could make out a pair of hands and five weather-beaten fingers. On the right hand, she wore an old gold ring with a large amber ruby in the middle. She had long, overgrown toenails on her feet.

'Do you have room and board for my friends here?' asked Luigi.

'That I do, Luigi. That I do. Hello...? Who is this young lady I see before me?' said the witch-doctor.

Bella moved back swiftly and hid behind her mother again.

'Who is this young lady?' said the witch-doctor. 'You are Bella, are you not?' she said.

'HOW DID YOU KNOW!?!' cried Bella.

'I knew you'd come. I predicted your arrival. I saw it in the foretelling,' said the witch-doctor.

Bella felt confused.

'I have to admit, you impressed even me with your cleverness. I mean, that bit where you escaped from Captain Greed by jumping into the sea and swimming off on the back of your companion...brilliant!' said the witch-doctor.

Bella looked stunned. 'But how...how on earth can you know that? You weren't even there.'

'These bogs provide me with all the knowledge I require,' said the witch-doctor, 'and in any case, I tend to keep a close eye on what Captain Greed is doing at any one time.'

'Why on earth would you do that?' said Bella. 'Don't you know that he stole our home, took us hostage on his ship, tried to kill my mother and me by making us walk the plank. And all this because he wanted more gold, on top of the gold he already makes as a landlord.'

'I care very deeply for him,' said the witch-doctor.

Bella thought this was very odd.

'Why would anyone care for a man so awful, so cruel, so...well... greedy, as a pirate like Captain Greed?'

'Because child,' said the witch-doctor, 'you see Captain Greed and I...well...this is going to come as a shock but...we're related to each other. I am his mother.'

Ten

The witch-doctor pushed open the door of her home. 'Come in, come in,' she said, asking her new companions to enter her home.

Bella was intrigued by what she found inside the witch-doctor's cottage. The house consisted of one room. In the centre of the room was a large cauldron containing a bubbling green liquid, like the kind of witches' brew Bella had read about in her bedtime stories at The Bell.

'Are you a witch?' said Bella.

'No dear, I'm a witch-doctor,' she said.

'You are not going to hurt us?' asked Bella.

'No dear,' said the witch-doctor. 'I don't hurt people or put curses on them. I just make potions to heal the sick, that's all. Although I can manipulate this cauldron, in order to reveal certain things. Pull up a chair and make yourselves comfortable.'

The trio pulled up three wooden chairs and sat in front of the cauldron. Bella immediately felt comfortable and in front of the warm fire, for a moment she was back in The Bell. She remembered being curled up next to Mum on a winter's night, having just eaten shepherd's pie for tea. How on earth could anyone live without this happiness? thought Bella.

'Did I hear you correctly, I thought you said that Captain Greed is your son?' said Doggie.

'Yes, that's correct,' said the witch-doctor. Bella noticed she was rummaging around her collection of potions.

'But how is that possible?' said Mum. 'I mean he's a pirate and you...you're...you're here. All alone. On this island.'

'But I haven't just been on this island, have I?' said the witch-doctor. The party stared at her, confused. 'You see, I used to be a pirate too. Ah, here it is. That's what I was looking for, my stirring stick.' The witch-doctor picked up a long spoon.

Bella leaned into the cauldron. The green substance inside was turning faster and faster and as if by magic, sparkles began to twinkle at the edge of the pot. Suddenly she could make out images in the swill – faces, streets, the wide blue ocean with a pirate ship somewhere – and she suddenly realised that she was about to learn the truth about Captain Greed, how the witch-doctor got stuck on her island, and why Captain Greed was so selfish and greedy.

'Come, come,' said the witch doctor. 'Pull your chairs closer to the fire and you will learn the truth.'

Eleven

The green swill in the cauldron began to move until the picture became fixed. The images were so clear it felt to Bella like she was watching television.

The place was London and the witch-doctor lived with her handsome husband in a big Victorian house in a pretty neighbourhood with cherry trees lining the street outside the home.

Bella could see a younger witch-doctor. This wasn't the old woman she was confronted with now. This lady was young, sporty and uncommonly pretty.

'We were called the Parson family,' said the witch-doctor; 'Captain Greed's real name is Tom. And this is the sorry tale about how my beautiful boy, Tom, grew into the brute Captain Greed.'

The family were sitting around about to eat Sunday lunch. The witch-doctor and Tom were sitting at the dinner table, when Daddy came in carrying the roast chicken. They sat down and started eating.

'The important thing to remember about Daddy,' said the witch-doctor, giving the swill another good turn with the strong spoon, 'is that he was a doctor, a proper one. He spent his entire day saving lives and it meant the world to him.'

Oh, right thought Bella as she stared into the swill.

'Daddy,' said young Tom, 'what's the best thing about being a pirate?'

Bella thought Tom was just a little younger than she was, maybe eight or nine.

'Nothing. There's nothing good about being a pirate,' said Daddy.

'Really?' said Tom. 'What about the adventure?'

'Adventure? Poppycock! Life is about hard work and saving lives, not any of this adventure rubbish,' said Daddy.

'But pirates can become very rich, they take all that gold,' said Tom.

'Gold isn't everything in life, Tom,' said Daddy.

'What about those splendid costumes they wear? All those lovely satin trousers, handsome red overcoats and posh leather boots?'

'Child,' said Daddy, 'one day you'll discover there is more to life than wearing handsome overcoats and getting very, very rich.'

'Well screw you then!' said Tom, spitting his food out. 'I'm going to pirate school in Jamaica when I'm older and you can't stop me.'

'WHAT!?!' bellowed Daddy. 'You'll do no such thing!'

'Yes, I will,' shouted Tom, the tears welling up in his eyes.

'The first thing you'll do is go to your room with no lunch followed by a nice hot bath. Then tomorrow you'll put your head down at school and work very hard. No adventure for you.'

Bella stepped back from the cauldron. She couldn't believe what she was seeing in front of her eyes. Bella turned to the witch-doctor and said, 'Do you mean to tell me all that the young Captain Greed wanted was a life of travel and adventure?'

'Yes,' said the witch-doctor. 'He liked the idea of getting rich. But what my precious child really, really, wanted, more than money, was travel and adventure.'

'What did you do after that horrible lunch?' said Bella.

'I went upstairs and comforted him for the rest of the afternoon,' said the witch-doctor.

'Did Tom ever repair his relationship with his father,' asked Mum.

'No, I'm afraid not,' said the witch-doctor, looking very sad. 'When he finished his education at 11, he saved up his pocket money and bought a ticket to travel on a pirate ship to Jamaica, where he enrolled in pirate school.'

'Was he happy there?' asked Bella.

'Why don't you see for yourself...' said the witch-doctor.

Twelve

The witch-doctor turned to the cauldron, and with a slight wave of the hand, commanded the swill to begin turning. Turning and turning in the black cauldron, the swill began sparkling, giving off many, many bright lights of pink and gold.

Eventually the swill began to settle, and Bella could make out more images in the cauldron. This time they were on a pirate ship. Not a sea-going pirate ship, a dry-dock vessel. One built for budding pirates to practise their buccaneering on before they could be trusted to take their first big step out into the big, wide world.

'Now boys!' bellowed the teacher manfully, his horrible fat tummy poking out of his white and blue striped shirt; 'Remember, when you are boarding another vessel, the most important thing to remember is to make lots of noise when attacking your enemy. Make sure you make lots of noise when you attack. OK boys. On the count of three. One...two...three...attack!'

Bella stood in horror at every scene that unfolded before her disbelieving eyes. A row of young boys, mostly the same age as Tom, ran forward attacking rubber dummies with their cutlasses. They were sharp too, each silver sword reflecting the dazzling light of the high Jamaican sun.

Each boy ran forward, screaming and shouting until they were red in the face. Bella thought to herself that their throats must hurt after all that shouting and those boys could do with some nice cough syrup to make sure they didn't do any damage to their vocal chords.

But there was one little boy who was not getting involved. He dropped his cutlass and sank to the floor, he put his knees up to his eyes and was rocking back and forth. Bella could see he was crying.

'Is that Tom?' said Bella.

'Yes,' said the witch-doctor.

Bella looked on in disbelief as the fat, red-faced teacher came towards the little boy.

'Now, now little lad. Young pirates shouldn't be crying,' said the teacher.

Young Tom wiped a tear from his eye. 'I just don't want to hurt anyone,' said Tom.

'Well, what did you expect pirate school to be? It's not all jam sandwiches and ice cream in pirate school you know,' said the teacher.

'And I miss my mum and dad,' said Tom.

'Well tough luck. You're here now so you'll just have to live with it,' said the teacher. After hearing that, poor Tom burst into tears again and immediately went to sit in the crow's nest.

'What a poor thing to put a little boy through. What did you do?' said Bella.

'Nothing. He sat in the crow's nest until graduation - where he got through as the worst performing pirate of his year group, and scraped by with a pass.'

'Why didn't you try to get him out of that horrible pirate school?' said Bella.

'We tried but we couldn't. The pirate school was totally separate. They wouldn't allow any home visits, any holidays or leave. There were no parents' evenings either. We weren't even allowed to write letters. It was a very happy day when Tom arrived home. Perhaps you're wondering how that went. Well, you can see for yourself...'

The witch-doctor made one quick motion of her hand and the swill began moving. This time the images offered up by the cauldron were of the same comfortable London home that Bella had witnessed a moment before.

The witch-doctor and Daddy were sitting at the kitchen table. Young Tom had been so beastly to them before leaving for pirate school in Jamaica. The witch-doctor was crying, and her husband was comforting her.

'What did we do wrong?' sniffed the witch-doctor through the tears.

'He's just a very selfish little boy,' said the husband; 'He's gone now and he's not coming back.'

Bella felt so sorry for that poor family. 'What did you do?' enquired Bella.

'I'll show you,' said the witch-doctor. 'We are about to see Captain Greed's first raid and discover the truth about how I ended up on this cursed island.'

Thirteen

'I travelled to the Spanish Main because I heard a rumour that Tom would be there,' said the witch-doctor, 'and found him outside a village on the coast, a little like the one where you and Mum live,' said the witch-doctor.

'I see,' said Bella.

'In order for this memory to be conjured up in the cauldron, we are going to need something special. This is a bad memory, so we need something extra strong for the cauldron to do its work, wait here.' The witch-doctor went over to a shelf and took down a jug with a cork in it with 'XXXX' written on the label.

'Yes, I think this will do very well,' said the witch-doctor. She opened the jug, poured out a handful of little red stones and tossed them into the cauldron.

'What's that you have there?' said Bella.

'Well, if I told you that would break the spell, wouldn't it?' asked the witch-doctor, 'look, the cauldron is doing its work.'

The images in the cauldron began turning and turning until they became fixed; a small coastal village, a young man wearing a large black hat, posh leather boots and a handsome red overcoat. He was brandishing a large cutlass and holding in his hand a grey bag heavy with gold. At his feet a woman was begging him.

'Well, I think this will do very well. I can buy myself a new ship with this lovely gold,' said Tom.

'But good pirate,' sobbed the woman, clasping her hands together, 'please don't take my dowry. That's all I have. If you take that away from myself and my children, we'll be penniless.'

'Sorry, my good woman, there's nothing I can do,' said Tom.

'But that gold is mine. I've worked all my life for that gold,' begged the woman.

'My dear lady, dry those eyes. If you consult the contract for this home, you'll see it belongs to me. You see it's right here in this paragraph,' said Tom, taking out a scroll of parchment. 'You see right here...' he said pointing a finger at a small clause at the bottom of the scroll of parchment. Bella, who was watching events unfold from the comfort of the witch-doctor's cottage, thought the writing was so small it was practically unreadable. With the best will in the world, thought Bella, no one could take that scroll seriously. 'You see, if you look there, it says that before this house was built, the land was owned by Pirates Incorporated, of which I am the Chief Pirate.'

The sentence was so small the homeless lady had to squint to read it. Then the poor woman began trembling. 'So this scroll makes you....it makes you...'

'...it makes me your landlord, yes,' said Tom.

'But where will we go?' said the woman. 'My children and I will have to travel the roads all along the Spanish Main begging for money from men from the British Navy who visit here from time to time.'

'You may end up doing that but as long as I'm getting rich then I don't care,' said Tom.

'You're a beast!' she cried.

'Correction: my name is Captain Greed,' and with that Tom took the bag of gold and boarded his ship.

'How can such a lovely little boy, who only wanted to do what he really wanted to do, turn into such a horrible, cruel and well....greedy pirate?'

'That's what the love of gold will do, little Bella. Try to understand Bella, Captain Greed is a bad pirate not because he wants to gain gold, but because he tried to use gold to make up for the lack of love in his life. You see after leaving home, Tom realised he had made a terrible mistake. He missed his mum and dad and felt sorry for being horrible to them before leaving for Jamaica. At some point he realised there was no love in his life, so he tried to replace love with gold. He thought that if he just became as rich as he possibly could, then everything would be alright. But he never forgot his mum and dad and he never forgot how cruel he had been to his poor parents. With the passing of the years, his guilt became greater. He robbed and stole more and more. At some point he decided to be cruel to other people in his pursuit of gold, and he didn't care about what he was doing to others, because if he did stop and think, he would see the people he's made poor and the children he's made homeless.'

'Witch-doctor,' said Bella, 'have you tried to stop Captain Greed and bring back your beloved Tom?'

'Yes,' said the witch-doctor. 'I tried. But he was having none of it. I went to the village on the Spanish Main, but he wouldn't let me board his ship. He wouldn't listen to a word I said and instead put this spell on me. Casting me out of our lovely home in London and instead banishing me to this godforsaken island. He forced me to live as a haggard old witch-doctor while my boy, my beautiful boy, is out there.'

'If there was a way of getting Tom back, breaking the spell and reuniting you with your son, would you help me do i"? said Bella.

'Yes, oh how I would love that.'

'In that case,' said Bella, 'I have an idea!'

Fourteen

Bella went upstairs and began rummaging around in the attic of the witch-doctor's cottage.

'No, that won't do at all,' Bella said to herself, tossing aside a leather jacket which she thought just didn't look right.

'Nope, this won't do either,' said Bella, throwing away a sword which wasn't sharp enough.

Two hours later Mum became hungry and sat down for dinner with the witch-doctor. Doggie woke from his sleep and realised that Bella was nowhere to be seen.

THUMP...!

Doggie heard the sound of a leather boot hitting the back of the attic door. His ears pricked up and he wondered what on earth must be going on up there. He went upstairs to investigate, suspecting that Bella was maybe in trouble. It was a tight squeeze, up there in the attic, it is not an easy job for a seven-foot dog to squeeze into the top of a witch-doctor's house.

'Bella, what on earth are you doing?' said Doggie, looking at the mess Bella had made in the attic. The floor was covered in old jackets, worn out old pirate boots, bits of old map, compasses, swords and other pirate things that were gathering dust in the attic.

'I'm busy,' said Bella.

'Busy?' said Doggie, 'doing what?'

'Gathering things together,' said Bella. 'You see Doggie, I have decided to become a pirate!'

'And why on earth would you want to go and do a thing like that?' asked Doggie.

'I was gazing at the cauldron, watching the sad story of poor Tom and how he became Captain Greed, when suddenly I had an idea.'

'Yesss...' said Doggie trying his best to disguise his worry.

'Well, if you can have selfish pirates, who bring misery to people in the Caribbean, why can't you have a pirate who brings goodness. If you can have a pirate for greed, why can't you have a pirate for kindness? I shall call myself Captain Kindness and go buccaneering on the high seas spreading joy and happiness across the world. I'll kick the landlords out of the Caribbean, force pirates to pay their taxes and return the properties taken by Greed to the villages.'

'That sounds wonderful,' said Doggie, 'and what's your ship going to be?'

Bella thought for a moment, 'Err...I haven't thought that far ahead to be honest. What about The Fluffy Roger?'

Doggie looked up at the ceiling in embarrassment. 'Err...I think that sounds...nice.'

'You don't like it?' said Bella, suspecting that Doggie wasn't being completely honest.

'I don't like the thought of a ship called The Fluffy Roger,' said Doggie.

'Ok, I will have a rethink,' said Bella.

'What's going on up there?' enquired a voice from downstairs.

Bella and Doggie heard footsteps on the stairs and they both knew instantly that Mum and the witch-doctor were coming upstairs.

Mum and the witch-doctor threw open the door to find Doggie and Bella surrounded by a mess of pirate clothes.

'What are you doing up here?' said Mum.

'Mum, I have decided to become a pirate. From now on, I am Captain Kindness. Dedicated to giving every family a home to live in and banishing forever the horrible pirate-landlords, who have caused so much misery to so many families.'

'Oh darling, that's wonderful. I'm so proud,' said Mum.

'I see. So that's what you've been doing up here in my attic. You've been rummaging around my old pirate clothes and equipment, haven't you?' said the witch-doctor. 'All this stuff - the hat, the maps and compasses - they are all Tom's pirate things. He left them with me when he went off to pirate school in Jamaica.'

'Witch-doctor, may I borrow Tom's pirate clothes?' asked Bella.

'Of course, you can,' said the witch-doctor. 'Take good care of them. What do you propose to do with Captain Greed?' she then asked.

'I have a plan for Captain Greed. But I need your help. Witch-doctor, you must come with me,' said Bella.

'I'm not looking forward to it. But if it will help rid the world of those pirates then I'll do it,' she said.

'Hooray!' said Doggie.

'Right, that's excellent, show me the way to the ship,' said the witch-doctor.

A terrible silence fell.

'Err...we don't have one,' said Bella.

'Oh, right,' said the witch-doctor. 'You'll have to find one quickly. Wait, I have an idea. Let's go to the beach. I have a plan to get you a ship and then you'll be able to take on Captain Greed and get my beloved son back. Come with me. The sun is high in the sky, and we absolutely must get to the sea before night fall.'

Fifteen

'Right, here we are. This is the edge of the Caribbean Ocean. Out there, Captain Greed is sailing around the world, and we have to stop him,' said Bella, looking out across the sea.

Bella was dressed head to foot, in the witch-doctor's old pirate clothes from the attic: a hat, a pair of boots and a waistcoat.

'But you still need a ship,' said the witch-doctor.

'Yes...err...I have to be honest. I'm a bit stuck when it comes to the ship,' said Bella.

'Right, let me think...' said the witch-doctor. 'Doggie, didn't you once say you were a navigator?'

'Yes, I was. It was one of the first things I told Bella when I met her in the brig of Captain Greed's ship. I used to be the navigator for Greed before the mutiny.'

'I see,' said the witch-doctor. 'Doggie, can you do me a favour? Please walk out into the ocean a bit. Not a great deal, just until the water starts to cover your tummy.'

'Alright,' said Doggie, feeling a bit silly but he went dutifully into the water anyway.

'A bit further...' said the witch-doctor.

Doggie felt this was very suspicious, but did as he was told anyway.

'A bit further...' said the witch-doctor. Now Doggie was very suspicious, but did as he was told anyway.

'Ok, stay there,' said the witch-doctor. Doggie was feeling very, very suspicious at what his friends were up to. The water was practically up to his ears by this point, and he wondered if he wasn't being used in some way he didn't quite understand. Unknown to him, because he was quite far away now and couldn't see properly, the witch-doctor was reaching into her back pocket for her wand.

'Witch-doctor, what are you doing....?' asked Bella.

'Don't worry, I know what I'm doing dear. Now, Doggie turn around...'

'You want me to turn around? Why?' said Doggie. By this time the friends were very, very far away from each other and Doggie had to shout to make himself heard.

'Doggie, do as I command,' shouted the witch-doctor. So, Doggie did as he was told and turned around until he was staring at the horizon.

'Right everyone, get ready and watch this,' whispered the witch-doctor. Bella wondered what on earth the witch-doctor had in store when, suddenly she pulled out her magic wand, flung it forward, the pointy end glowed bright green and IMMEDIATELY a bolt of bright green light zapped forward hitting Doggie square on the nose. There was a great confusion of bright lights and loud sounds and suddenly Doggie was transformed into a Pirate Ship!

'You cruel beast, what have you done to Doggie!' said Bella, very upset at seeing her friend turned into a pirate ship.

'Don't worry Bella, it's perfectly safe. I've just put a spell on Doggie for a little while. He's perfectly alright, I promise.'

'All aboard!' cried Doggie. Everyone climbed aboard and they were on their way.

'Wait a minute,' said Bella. 'I've just thought of something, where is Luigi?'

'Oh. Luigi is not here today,' said the witch-doctor. 'He's transformed himself into a bat.'

'He's transformed himself into a bat?' said Bella.

'Yes. Vampires can do that sort of thing. Protects himself from the sunlight that way. You see, sunlight can't hurt him if he's a bat. Don't worry too much, Bella, I have a feeling that Luigi will have a very important part to play in our story.'

Sixteen

'Avast!' cried Captain Greed gazing through his telescope, which he pointed towards the sky. 'What's that up there able seaman?'

The able seaman put his hand over his eyes to shield them from the burning sun. 'It would appear to be some sort of...bat, Captain.'

'A bat? What in blue blazes are you talking about man?' said Captain Greed. 'Bats usually hang around dark caves and people's basements. There's no account of bats out here on the wide blue ocean.'

'Well, Captain, there may be no accounts of bats at sea in the library of the pirate council, but that is definitely a bat.'

The bat swung low over the ship. It was high noon, the hottest time of the day. There was no wind so the disgusting black sails were rolled up. The ship was moving nowhere.

'When will the wind return?' enquired Greed.

'I have no idea Captain,' replied the able seaman.

The lack of movement was the least of the Captain's worries. The crew were becoming restless. After so many days and nights at sea, questions were being asked about Captain Greed's claims. There were rumours that all this business about a magic cave in Panama might not actually be true. It might, some pirates said, just be an excuse for Captain Greed to hide as much of his money as possible. Perhaps, the crew whispered to each other over their bread and cheese in the evening, that the Captain had, in fact, made the whole thing up.

'If Captain Greed really does have a magic cave,' said one pirate to another, 'why won't he tell us exactly where it is?'

'Greed promised us more gold, an extra ration of grog and better sleeping conditions on the ship. What happened?' said another pirate, helping himself to another cup of grog.

'Greed promised my wife and children a nice flat to rent, with a new dishwasher. He still hasn't provided one,' said a third.

The bank the Captain insisted on using to keep the gold they plundered was also causing suspicion. The pirates began to suspect that this so-called bank might in fact be a hoax for the Captain to hold on to as much of the gold as possible. Captain Greed was becoming nervous that, if he wasn't careful, he would have another mutiny on his hands.

'A SHIP!' cried the pirate who was sitting in the crow's nest. 'A ship is on the horizon, Captain.'

It was Bella, Mum, the witch-doctor, and Doggie, now, through the witch-doctor's incredible magic, transformed into a ship capable of transporting them all over the seas.

Captain Greed looked at the party through his telescope and gasped in horror. 'But what...how...it's that girl who was very rude to me,' he said. Greed noticed there was a third person amongst the party, an old woman in a black cloak, whom he didn't recognise. Greed stared at them and said to himself, '...but how did they...how did they LIVE?'

The able seaman shrugged his shoulders. Greed glanced up again at the bat who was circling overhead.

'It's that infernal bat,' said Captain Greed. 'That creature has led them right to us. Don't ask me how, but I just know for sure.'

By now Doggie was pulling up alongside Greed's ship.

'Prepare to be boarded!' cried Bella, like the pirates in the best stories Mum used to read to her at bedtime in The Bell. Her mother saw her daughter face the mean pirates, and she thought her very courageous. That was Bella's secret, courage. Even at the darkest of times, she never lost her confidence. The courage to face up to a greedy pirate landlord, the courage to apprehend a pirate ship. Her little girl had certainly come a long way since the days when she was bullied by Raymond. Even when that loyalty put her own safety at risk, she was always there. It takes courage to love your family like that.

'I cast thee frozen in time,' said the witch-doctor and thrust her wand forward. A bolt of green light came out of the witch-doctor's wand and zipped around every member of the crew.

Immediately every member was frozen on the spot.

'We're coming aboard,' said Bella. She grabbed a length of the rigging and swung over to where Captain Greed was standing. Captain Greed looked very worried indeed.

'But Bella...how did you survive? I saw you drop into the ocean,' said Captain Greed.

'You forgot that Doggie was an expert swimmer,' said Bella.

'Curses!' said Greed. He looked Bella up and down. 'You're very strangely dressed. Why do I get the feeling I've seen those clothes before Bella?'

'My name is Captain Kindness, and I am here to spread kindness, forgiveness, tolerance, and loveliness across the whole Caribbean. And you, Captain Greed, should be grateful I am here because you need me to put you straight about one or two matters.'

By now Captain Greed was blushing bright red like a tomato. He was absolutely dumbstruck and didn't know what to say.

'You see, Greed, after we escaped your ship, I happened to bump into your mother and she told me the whole sorry story. About how you desperately wanted to go to pirate school but weren't allowed. Well, we've talked it over and we've all agreed that now is probably the time to stop taking it out on others. We know you were disappointed at the time, but that doesn't give you the right to make other people's lives a misery. You've been greedy and very selfish. Now, we think the kindest thing to do to you is to have a very frank and honest conversation with yourself,' said Bella.

Captain Greed looked very sad.

Then Mum began to pipe up. She said, 'What Bella is saying, is you must stop being so awful to the towns and villages on the coast. They did not stop you achieving your ambition, or contribute to your humiliation, so they don't deserve to be made poor and homeless. You've also got this thing my mum calls attitude, so stop it.'

'And what do you think is going to persuade me to do that?' said Greed.

'Well, there is someone I would like you to meet,' said Bella.

The little gathering parted, and a small, frail woman came forward. She was the witch-doctor, Captain Greed's mother. 'Tom...Tom...it's me. It's your mother. I have frozen your crew in time so we can have a little talk without being interrupted.'

'Mum,' said Greed.

'Tom, I am so very, very, sorry, I didn't stand up to your brute of a father. He was mean, selfish and above all, unkind. But it was a very, very long time ago and you stealing from every island in the Caribbean won't change the past. If you love me, give away all your gold and go and do good works from now on.'

'Oh Mum,' said Greed. 'What a selfish old pirate I have been. Of course, I will. Let's go home. Bella, Mum, please forgive me for making you walk the plank. You may have The Bell back, would you like a lift home?'

'Oh yes,' said Mum.

'Let's go home Mum,' said Greed. 'But before we unfreeze the crew. I just have to sign this document giving back all my gold.'

Seventeen

It was supper time in The Bell. The old men of the sea were happy and had hungrily devoured one of the shepherd's pies made by Bella's mother. Mum baked the pies in the new oven she had bought with the money Captain Greed gave her to apologise for kidnapping her and taking her away. The Bell too had been given a lick of paint. The town was peaceful and prosperous, and everybody was happy. The horrible night when the pirates came seemed like nothing more than a bad dream. If the old men of the sea came into The Bell and talked about the time when the town was invaded by pirates, with a ship so large it blacked out the moon, it was to laugh and smile. Everyone agreed it was a long time ago and they could move on. It was a long time ago.

Bella, Mum and Doggie, now returned to his ordinary state as a dog, were sitting around the fireplace enjoying a hot cup of cocoa.

'It was awfully nice of the witch-doctor to turn me back to normal,' said Doggie.

'And it's awfully nice of you to join the family Doggie,' said Mum. 'Speaking of which, there's someone I want you to meet,' and she gave a whistle. There was a sound of a small creature moving in the next room. Bella heard paws on the floor next door. The little steps became louder and louder. Then they heard the door opening and four legs on the pub floor...

COCO!

Coco had been waiting for them while they were away on their adventure.

'Oh Coco, my beloved dog!' said Bella. 'Where have you been?'

'She's been living with a neighbour while we've been out of the town on our adventure,' said Mum.

'I'm so happy,' said Bella, who briefly put down the book she was writing in.

'What are you doing, Bella?' asked Mum

'I'm writing a book. I want to call it *Captain Kindness*. It's about a pirate who sails across the high seas spreading, love, joy and happiness to everyone.'

'That sounds absolutely wonderful darling,' said Mum. 'Oh, by the way, did I tell you I bumped into Raymond's mother in the market the other day?'

'No,' said Bella.

'Well, I did, and do you know what, since you asked Raymond to come to your birthday party, he's been much better in class. Paying more attention, answering more questions and his mother says he's been very helpful and kind around the house.'

'Well done Raymond,' said Bella.

'See what wonders a little kindness can do?' said Mum.

'I know, isn't it amazing,' said Bella. 'Mum, do you know the most important thing I've learned on our adventure?'

'No, what is it?' asked Mum.

'I think kindness will solve most of the problems in the world. Some people work very hard to make themselves happy. Showing an unhappy person a little bit of kindness will solve most people's problems. Like Captain Greed, he stole from the poor and robbed his crew of their wages and charged massive rents to people because he was really, really, unhappy and all the gold in the Caribbean wouldn't have changed his spirit.'

'That's very true, Bella. By the way, how is Captain Greed these days?'

'I received a letter in the post from him,' said Bella

'Oh really,' said Mum.

'Yes,' said Bella. 'I have it here with me. Would you like me to read it?'

'Yes, please,' said Mum.

'It goes: Dear Bella. I'm so happy that you reunited me with my mother. I can't thank you enough for taking all that trouble to do something so kind. I've sold my ship and bought my mother a large house. The house is very nice, and not the kind of damp, dank, smelly place I used to let people rent from me. But a proper house with a large garden and everything. I've also found the whole crew jobs elsewhere and haven't thrown them out without jobs to go to. My mother and I are really very happy here. I've also found a proper job at a bank. I pay my money to the taxman and don't hide my money selfishly away. I make an honest living and don't lie, cheat or steal anymore.'

'Well, that's wonderful,' said Mum.

On they went, talking late into the night. They talked about the lessons they had learned together, and how they could spread kindness and healing to even more people. They also agreed that Captain Greed was right to pay taxes. By keeping the money he stole from the people, he was really robbing his crew, and that he was right to put a stop to this. They talked about how grateful they were for their family, until eventually, the conversation came round to the subject of Captain Greed's clothes; the posh leather boots and red coat which he had taken so much pride in and had wanted so badly.

'He also mentioned his pirate clothes in his letter,' said Bella.

'Yes...' said Mum.

'His posh boots and the like. He threw them away. He said he doesn't need them anymore.'

'Well, I think there's a lesson in there for all of us. Now, Bella, would you like another helping of shepherd's pie?'

...and they all lived happily ever after.

THE END